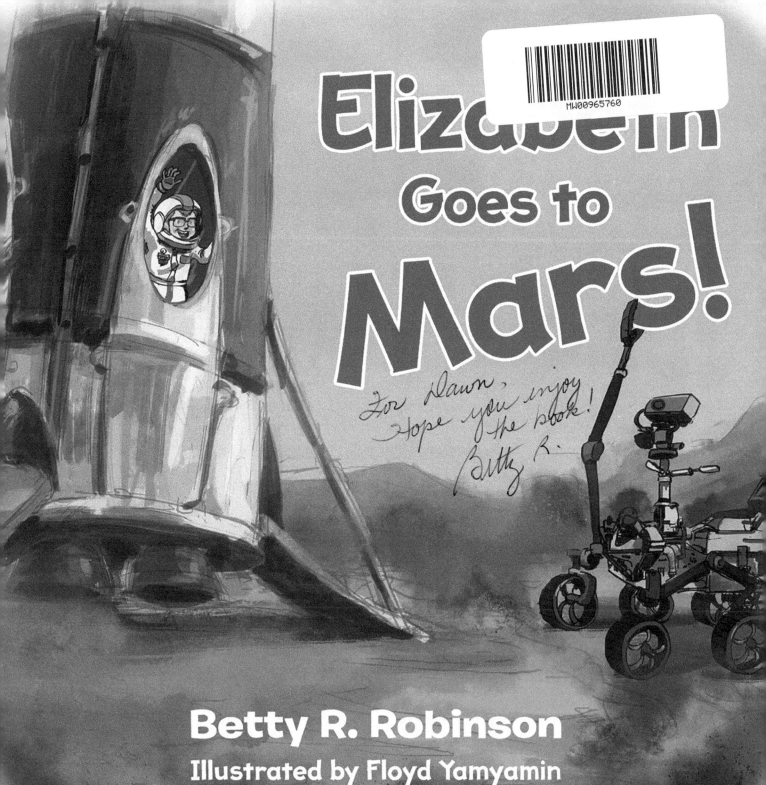

Elizabeth Goes to Mars!

For Dawn,
Hope you enjoy
the book!
Betty R.

Betty R. Robinson
Illustrated by Floyd Yamyamin

Elizabeth Goes to Mars!
Copyright © 2020 by Betty R. Robinson

Tellwell Talent
www.tellwell.ca

ISBN
978-0-2288-2811-2 (Hardcover)
978-0-2288-2810-5 (Paperback)
978-0-2288-4130-2 (eBook)

For Beth and Randy

Ken on TV: "Hello, viewers. We are back with our space expert, Randy, talking about going to Mars. Randy, you've described how desolate Mars is—it's cold, there's no liquid water and no atmosphere to speak of, so no air for us to breathe. There are lots of dust storms that can clog solar panels. And it's going to be challenging to grow plants for food. Now, let's talk about the actual trip to Mars and the challenges of just getting there!"

Randy: "Sure, Ken. First of all, it's a long, lonely, boring trip to Mars, about eight to nine months. Astronauts will have to bring all their own food, water, and medicine. And radio communication is SLOW because Mars is so far away."

Randy: "One of the most serious dangers is radiation from the Sun. Once we are far away from Earth, we won't be protected by Earth's magnetic field. Our magnetic field blocks harmful radiation from the Sun. Without that protection, the exposure to the harmful radiation is very dangerous for the people in the spacecraft. And of course, Mars doesn't have a global magnetic field.

"Basically, the more mass, or material, between the radiation from the Sun and the astronauts, the better. The spacecraft will protect us to a certain degree. We can't add thick walls to the spacecraft because that adds too much weight, which means more fuel. Once astronauts get to Mars, some habitats could be built into the Martian hills."

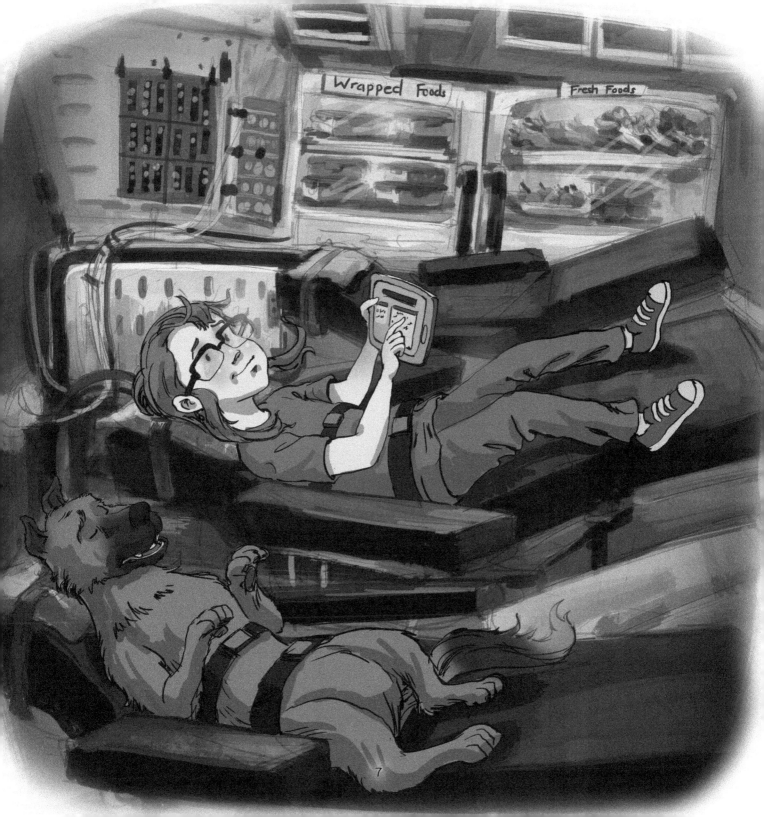

Elizabeth: "I just did this yesterday! And the day before. And the day before that! Why do I have to keep doing this all the time?"

Mom: "If you don't keep exercising, you're going to lose some of your bone strength. As long as we aren't on Earth, we have to keep exercising every day!"

Elizabeth: "Mom! There's *Curiosity*. Why is *Curiosity* here? You said our habitat latitude is about 40° in the northern hemisphere, but *Curiosity* always works just below the equator, in the southern hemisphere."

Mom: "*Curiosity* is retired now. After many, many years of working on Mars, *Curiosity* is a senior citizen. Other robots have taken over her job. She is now a goodwill ambassador, welcoming everyone to Mars."

Elizabeth: "Wow, the sky is so orangey! And it's August on Earth, so it's summer at home on Earth. But it's summer here too, right? It's kind of dark yet there are no clouds. No trees, just reddish soil and rocks. Why is it so different here?"

Mom: "So far, there is no evidence of life on Mars. So no vegetation.

"Mars is farther away from the Sun than Earth, and it only gets about 40% of the energy we get on Earth.

"It takes longer for Mars to go around the Sun because its orbit is larger. A Martian year is around 687 Earth days, compared to an Earth year of 365 days. So, the seasons are longer on Mars.

"Also, the path that Earth takes around the Sun is almost a circle. The path that Mars takes around the Sun is more oval, kind of like a slightly flattened circle. And with this different shape, the seasons are different lengths, while on Earth the seasons are similar in length.

"Here in the Martian northern hemisphere, summer lasts almost 180 Martian days. And a winter lasts almost 155 Martian days. Actually, we are getting close to the autumnal equinox. Summer on Mars this year started around the end of March, and fall starts near the end of September."

Elizabeth: "Pizza?! How can we have pizza on Mars?"

Mom: "Well, before any people arrived on Mars, all the supply missions brought tools, materials, canned foods, freeze-dried foods, and more, like flour. We do have to learn to be self-sufficient and grow as much food as possible. Like wheat—we can grow a type of wheat here in the plant houses, but it takes a *lot* of wheat plants to produce enough flour.

"And it's not that difficult to make the dough. It just takes practice in this reduced-gravity environment, especially when using the ovens. The gravity on Mars is a little over one-third of the gravity on Earth, so everything is different—preparing the foods, boiling water, cooking the foods. We grow tomatoes here. We will visit the gardens tomorrow. The cheese is freeze-dried from home.

"Plus, I know you don't mind not eating meat. Unless meat comes on a supply mission, we have to do without. Sorry, Rigel!"

Elizabeth: "So weird! On Earth, we have a blue sky during the day and a reddish sky at sunset. On Mars, it's the opposite.

"But I think I know why. Sunlight is made of different colours. Like the rainbow. The colours are different wavelengths of light. On Earth, the longer wavelengths of light, such as red, pass right through the molecules in the atmosphere. But the molecules absorb the shorter wavelengths of light, such as blue. Then the molecules send the blue light around the sky.

"On Mars, there's hardly any atmosphere at all. The red dust on Mars makes the sky look reddish during the day. And at night it can look bluish near the Sun. Tiny water ice particles in high clouds scatter the blue light."

Elizabeth: "Look, there are the two moons! They are pretty small compared to our Moon. The brighter moon is Phobos, and the other moon is Deimos. They are named after two soldiers in Greek mythology who fought with their father, Ares, the God of War.

"Phobos is bright but not super bright. Look—we have a bit of a shadow, but not much."

Elizabeth: "Wait a minute... the constellations look the same from Mars as they do from Earth. I guess that's because stars are just *so far* away compared to the distances to the planets, so how they look doesn't seem to change. One thing has changed, though: the stars aren't twinkling! Right–no atmosphere to speak of on Mars like we have on Earth, so no twinkling.

"I know that Mars doesn't have a north star, like we do. Just by chance, our Earth axis points to Polaris. But Mars' axis points to an area between Deneb in the constellation Cygnus and Alderamin, in the constellation Cepheus."

Elizabeth: "I understand how we can have so many lights on Mars. We can use solar panels to convert energy from the Sun into useful energy, like heat and light. But what about those different colours of light in the plant house we saw the other day? Here comes Swapnil. He will know because he works in the plant house."

Elizabeth: "I see different types of gardens here. Why are there different colours of LEDs? And apart from the reduced amount of sunlight, what makes it tough to grow plants here?"

Swapnil: "Several scientists on Earth, including a team of Canadians—I know you're Canadian—did a lot of research on growing plants on Mars. We learned that certain types of plants respond better to certain wavelengths of light in non-Earth environments. Look at this red-leaf lettuce. We are growing some lettuce with white light, some lettuce with red light, and some lettuce with blue light. Look how different they are. And they are growing without dirt. We only give them fertilizer and water.

"The other big problem is pressure. These plants evolved on Earth. So, they are used to a certain amount of light, food, water, and atmospheric pressure. With very little atmospheric pressure on Mars, the plants don't understand; they respond by going into drought mode. But even when we add more water, it doesn't help enough. So, we have to increase the pressure inside the plant house just enough so the plants can survive."

Elizabeth: "What's going on over there? That's a lot of big machinery."

Mom: "That's how we get our water, which also gives us our oxygen to breathe, by the way. The soil in this area at this latitude has a lot of water in it, in the form of ice. That's why we're so far from the equator, where it's a little warmer.

"The excavator digs up the soil. We then heat the soil by microwaves. Soon the water in the soil changes to water vapour, which rises. But then once the water vapour cools, it condenses into liquid water. Then we collect the liquid water and store it. And we recycle the water as much as possible.

"Do you remember from science class that water is made of hydrogen and oxygen? Once we have the water, we can extract the oxygen and use it in our living areas."

Elizabeth: "Yikes! Look at that dust storm. What do we do?"

Mom: "No problem. We just get back to base. Now."

Elizabeth: "This dust clogs up the solar panels so they cannot convert solar energy into electrical energy. I'm glad that dust storm was short. I hear that sometimes Mars gets a dust storm so big it can cover the planet for a few weeks. Good thing we have those batteries for emergencies and for nighttime."

Ken on TV: "Randy, we're just about out of time now. Thank you for sharing your thoughts on going to Mars. Anything quick you'd like to add?"

Randy: "My pleasure, Ken. We have talked about just a few of the challenges we will face when we go to Mars. But human beings are explorers. We are driven by curiosity about potential life beyond our planet. We want to understand how the planets formed. The more we understand, then the more we can learn about Earth. And Mars seems to be the most habitable planet apart from Earth. We will get to Mars. But let me leave you with this: would you like to visit Mars?"

CPSIA information can be obtained
at www.ICGtesting.com
Printed in the USA
BVHW021928040621
608856BV00002B/29

9 780228 828105